Jasmine
Fitting In!

Samantha Rugen lives with her fiancé in Liverpool.
She teaches in a primary school as well as illustrating and
writing books. This is her fourth book for Piccadilly.

Also available by Samantha Rugen, from Piccadilly Press:
Everything a Girl Should Know
Getting a Life
More to Getting a Life

Jasmine - Fitting In!

Samantha Rugen

Piccadilly Press • London

And finally . . . for David!

Printed and bound by Creative Print and Design (Wales),
Ebbw Vale, for the publishers Piccadilly Press Ltd.
5 Castle Road, London NW1 8PR

Set in Futura Book, 10 pt

A catalogue record for this book is available
from the British Library

ISBNs: 1 85340 650 3 (trade paperback)
1 85340 645 7 (hardback)

1 3 5 7 9 10 8 6 4 2

Cover design by Jessica Meserve

AUGUST

Sunday, Aug. 29th, 5.00 p.m.

I just can't believe it. We are actually here. This is real. This is our new 'home'. I keep thinking, Why did Mum do this to us? We didn't have to come here. She didn't have to take the job. Don't we matter? She's dragged us hundreds of miles from everything and everyone and has totally ignored our feelings. She doesn't listen and she doesn't care. She is *so* selfish! Can't she see she's wrecking our lives? I just can't believe we are here. I want to go home.

Monday, Aug. 30th, 11.00 p.m.

There is no way I am staying here. I'm going back home. I'll give it a week, then I'm ringing Dad. I don't care if I do upset Mum! She can't really expect me to stay. She knew I'd hate it here, but she still made me come. How can she expect us to live here? Why didn't Dad argue with her more? I miss him already. He didn't want us to move away. I could've stayed with him and Kay. I could've helped look after the baby when it comes. He could've convinced Mum she'd get a promotion back home if she'd waited a few more years. She was bound to get the Editor's job eventually.

I thought Dad might have rung by now, even if Mum did ask him to wait until we'd 'settled in'. He should know I need him now.

Tuesday, Aug. 31st, 9.00 a.m.

Another sleepless night. I thought I might cry myself to sleep. I didn't. I lay awake all night and listened. Listened to the noises a huge, strange house makes in the dark. Listened to Dylan sobbing. Listened to Poppy unpacking as though this is the best thing that's ever happened. Listened to traffic and voices outside. The city is a noisy place all right! There's just no way I can stay here.

SEPTEMBER

Wednesday, Sept. 1st, 2.35 p.m.

I must've actually gone to sleep last night, even if for only a short time. When I woke up, I thought I was back home for a few seconds. Then I remembered. I wasn't home. I was here. I am still here. I feel sick thinking about it. This is it! I am going to be waking up here for ever. In this huge, strange house. Even my own bed seems different here. I wonder if it will ever feel like home?

Thursday, Sept. 2nd, 8.10 p.m.

With the exception of my crystals, I still haven't unpacked. I've just had a row with Mum and told her that I'm not going to either! She always treats me like a kid! Dad doesn't. When I told Mum that I wanted to live with him, she completely ignored me and said she'd started looking for schools for me and Dylan! (I've spent so much time wiping away Dylan's tears that I could be a professional nose-blower! Between the two of us, we've cried buckets.) She's wasting her time, but she won't listen. She never does. Poppy's as bad! She told me I should go with Mum to help her choose! Poppy, my only sister, is even turning on me! The one person in the world I thought I could rely on! She told me to stop sulking and get on with it. I hate this place!

Friday, Sept. 3rd, 7.30 a.m.

I couldn't sleep again. My head was spinning and poor Dylan was sobbing. I went into his room and snuggled up with him, but once he fell asleep his snoring kept me awake! Eventually I went downstairs to make a drink. This house is so creepy. Even with all the lights on I still felt edgy! Back home, I could walk around with my eyes closed and not bump into a thing, but here . . .

Then I heard footsteps and completely panicked! I could feel my heart beating in my chest! I was relieved to see it was Poppy and not Mum. (We had *another* argument today.) I asked if I'd woken her, but she ignored me! I can't remember the last time she did that. Poppy never holds grudges. When I asked what her problem was she told me. And boy, did she tell me! She called me selfish and immature – amongst other things! I reminded her that I was only thirteen after all, but that made her worse. She said that no one had wanted to move and it felt like the end of the world to her too, but we have to make the most of it for Mum's sake. She asked if I really thought Mum would have made a decision to uproot and upset the entire family if she didn't think it was in our best interests. Then she went to bed. I eventually fell asleep in front of the television. Maybe she has got a point.

Saturday, Sept. 4th, 2.30 p.m.

I feel terrible. Poppy's right. I've been acting like a total brat. I've done nothing to help; I've sulked day and night; I've cried continuously – I've made poor Mum's life hell, really. I suppose I have been giving her a worse time than normal. I am proud of her getting this new job and I know she didn't take it without thinking things through first. It's just that everything has happened so quickly. I never imagined we'd ever move. Why should I? It was where I was born and where I lived for my entire life. I was happy there.

I felt so guilty this morning that I actually went downstairs for breakfast. The atmosphere was stony to say the least. I could tell Mum was still furious with me by the way she kept slamming doors and banging things! I decided to say sorry. Once I started to tell her how I felt, I couldn't hold back the tears! I was crying hysterically when I noticed Mum had started blubbering too. My emotional outburst was more than slightly overshadowed by this! I didn't know what to do at first. I felt really awkward! Mums aren't supposed to cry. She was so upset! I eventually hugged her for the first time in ages. We cried together for a good few minutes and I felt so much better. I think Mum did too. The last time I can remember her crying was when she and Dad told us they were getting divorced. Actually, that was mild compared to this. (After all, that was a mutual decision and definitely the right thing to do for both of them. I think she cried then more out of relief than anything else.)

In a strange way though, it was amazing! Mum was talking to me like an adult. She explained what a strain this whole move has been for her and that she never wants to make a decision like it again. She said she felt guilty because she knew how upset we were; that we must hate her for uprooting us all and dragging us to the other end of the country; for making us leave everything behind. But Dad made her realise this promotion was her chance of a lifetime. He convinced her it was the right decision to make, even if it took us all a long time to realise it.

I can't believe it! Dad was the one who made her decide! He told her we should go. It must've nearly killed him to say that! He said he never saw enough of us when he moved out – and then he was only a ten-minute walk away. Now he'll be seeing even less of us but he still wanted us to go. I'm not sure how I feel now. I can't believe he'd just let us go like that. Maybe now Kay's having a baby he wants a new start, a new family without us in the picture. No. I'm just being paranoid. I'm sure of it. He'd never do that. No. He wouldn't. Whatever, I don't know if it's made me feel better or worse, knowing that it's because of Dad's influence on Mum that we're here.

3.30 p.m.

I'm going to get over this! Stop being such an idiot, Jaz! Maybe I've been suffering from some kind of personality disorder brought on by stress! (I'm sure I read that moving house is as stressful as a death!) But I've got to try to be more like my old self again. No more of this self-pity stuff. Apart from anything else, it can't be healthy carrying around all this anger. And to think Carmel used to call me the eternal optimist! I'll try to start thinking happy thoughts from now on. I can feel my karma and aura becoming more positive by the second!

Sunday, Sept. 5th, 11.35 a.m.

What a job unpacking is! I feel like I've done a marathon. I'm exhausted. OK. I still hate this place. But, seeing the positive side, as the old Jaz would, I have to admit that I do have the most fabulous room in the history of bedrooms! And it's all mine! No more sharing with Dylan! It's only just starting to sink in. I'll admit to actually missing his snoring at first, but now I'm really appreciating the privacy. There's so much space for me to fill! I'm going to have to work out a decent colour scheme if I'm staying. The pink roses on this wallpaper must have driven the previous occupier to floral distraction!

I feel much better today. Mum's more like her old self again too. She's a bit stressed out thinking about her first day at work though. Poppy and I are going to make lunch and take Dylan for a walk so she can get herself sorted. She started ringing around a few decorators this morning. I think it was to take her mind off things. She's going to call some schools this week too. She's decided on a couple she thinks sound good, and wants us to look at them together. Eek! The thought of it sends shivers down my spine.

I said that of course I would go. After all, I'm doing my best impression of the perfect daughter at the moment. And when all is said and done, I've got no choice!

4.20 p.m.

We've just got back from our walk. Considering this is the city, it's a lovely, leafy area. It still feels weird though. I had a chance to have a good talk with Poppy. I apologised again for being such a brat and asked her if she knew about Dad's involvement in the decision to move. She didn't, but wasn't really surprised. When I told her what I had thought when I first heard, she said I was being paranoid. She reminded me what a sacrifice it must have been for him to make. I know she's right. He does love us more than anything in the world and the new baby won't change that. It won't be someone to be jealous of and be in competition with, but a new sister or brother. I love Poppy. She's such a cool sister.

9.40 p.m.

Dad's just rung. I can still feel a lump in my throat. I miss him! I still want to be back there with him and my friends! He was so upset speaking to us all. I could hear it in his voice. I didn't want to make it worse, so I swallowed hard. I'm quite proud of myself, actually. I held the tears back well. I told him everything was fine, but he said that he knew it would be a long time before I could say that and really mean it. He told me he loved me and missed me. Poppy was right; I was just being paranoid. This is harder for Dad than it is for us.

We were all quiet for a long time afterwards. I think Mum went for a little cry. I didn't. I wanted to, but I've done enough of that. Much as it hurts me to say, this is my new home. I'm just going to have to get used to it. We all are.

Monday, Sept. 6th, 10.15 a.m.

Mum looked a nervous wreck when she set out for work this morning. I'd probably feel the same. In fact, I will next Monday! A new school. Oh god. My stomach turns just thinking about it! I won't know a single person! All I keep thinking is that Carmel and everyone back home will be getting ready for a new term without me. Why can't things stay the same for ever? Life would be much easier then. But boring too, I suppose.

Tuesday, Sept. 7th, 12.10 p.m.

We had a fabulous meal last night. Mum took us into town to celebrate her first day! She was so excited, telling us all about it! Dad was right in making her take this job. After watching her last night, I know it was the right thing to do. We had a lovely time. It was the first time since we came here that we all laughed.

The city centre is huge. I'm quite looking forward to spending some pocket money there, actually! As we drove home, we stopped outside some tall gates. I wondered why we'd stopped – then I spotted the words 'Comprehensive School'. I felt sick. I have never seen such a massive building! It's awesome! How can I possibly go there? It looks like a prison!

How will I ever fit in here? So much for my positive thinking! I'm going to have to sleep with my calming rose quartz crystals under my pillow tonight, that's for sure!

Wednesday, Sept. 8th, 5.00 p.m.

I'm halfway through unpacking my last box. It's made things feel all final. The mountain of belongings in the hallway is disappearing slowly as they are placed in their new homes, and some decorators came to give us an estimate. Poppy's been out looking at colleges every day until today. She decided to 'have a day off' and hung around the house instead. I'm sure it was just because she'd laid eyes on Brad, the gorgeous blond painter. She is such a flirt!

I've told Mum that I want to decorate my room myself. I've got a few ideas already. It should take my mind off school, anyway. I'm desperate to ring Carmel and tell her all about what's going on. But on the other hand I'm dreading it. I want to hear all her news from back home, but can't bear to think of life carrying on there without me. This has been a very strange week. My planetary alignment must be going crazy!

Thursday, Sept. 9th, 2.30 p.m.

Oh god. We visited the school. We even got the bus there so I'd be familiar with the route. What an ordeal that's going to be, getting a bus to school! I'll have to leave the house half an hour earlier than I used to! And the thought of fighting for a seat every morning. God help me!

The whole thing was terrifying. The school is huge and there is actually CCTV in the playground! It is literally like a prison, with bars on the windows and intercoms everywhere! Inevitably, we got lost. An extremely spotty boy, whose accent I could hardly understand, directed us to the office. The place is like a rabbit-warren! There are hundreds of corridors! We finally found where we were supposed to be, and met the deputy head teacher. She seemed nice enough but I can hardly remember anything she said. I think I must've been in a state of shock! When she asked me a question, my mind went blank. I felt like I was having an out-of-body experience! I could barely string a sentence together. Amazingly, she told Mum she'd love to have me in the school. I start on Monday. I wish I were dead.

Friday, Sept. 10th, 10.00 a.m.

Poppy has been left in charge of taking Dylan and me to look for school uniforms! Cool! I can't believe Mum won't be taking us herself. I think she's already realising that 'new job' means working very long hours.

6.30 p.m.

Well. We're back after a successful shopping spree. The shops here are fantastic! I would've enjoyed the experience more if I hadn't been looking for the most hideous school uniform in the entire world. Lime green does nothing for me! And it's so stiff and uncomfortable, and so smart! I'll stick out like a sore thumb. I'll look like the new kid as soon as I walk through those gates – and I'll be an instant target for bullies. Help!

Saturday, Sept. 11th, 10.45 a.m.

I'm depressed. (What's new?) I got a good luck card from Carmel and everyone. She's sent me a lucky stone pendant. It's gorgeous. I'm wearing it now. It made me cry and I'd been doing really well until then, too. I've been putting a brave face on things for Dylan. He's been having panic attacks about going to a new school too, poor thing.

It's so weird. Reading Carmel's letter it sounds like life back home is just the same as ever. What I'd give to be back there; to be comfortable again; to have friends again; to be plain old Jaz again. I know one thing though. There's no way I'm going to let myself be a bully magnet again. Estelle Nugent made mine and Carmel's lives a misery last year. I'm not going to let history repeat itself here. I can handle being 'the weird, brainy, hippy kid'. I just don't fancy being 'the new kid' as well. No. I've made up my mind. I'm going to make friends here, even if it kills me! And at least then I can have a life. I've just read through my diary of the past few weeks. All that's happened in my life is this move! I want to have some fun again!

Sunday, Sept. 12th, 11.57 p.m.

Oh god. I hope I meet someone nice tomorrow. Someone who'll take pity on me and show me the ropes! With a bit of luck, Mum and Dad will be right and it won't be half as bad as I'm expecting it to be. I hope I get to sleep soon too! I've been rubbing my crystals and all my fingers are crossed! I just want tomorrow to be over as quickly as possible.

Monday, Sept. 13th, 9.50 p.m.

Today was the longest day of my life! And I've got to do it all again tomorrow! Not only was it a bad hair day, but I looked like the living dead after roughly three hours' sleep. We were running late and it was only when we were in the car – Mum wanted to take both Dylan and me herself on our first day – that I realised that I'd left my lucky pendant in the bathroom. I should've known that was an omen!

Things went from bad to worse. The car broke down and we waited for what felt like hours for the mechanic, with Dylan crying that he needed the toilet. Once we were on our way again, Mum took a wrong turning and we ended up stuck in a one-way system. Our little detour would have been the perfect sightseeing excursion of our new home town, if it hadn't been for the fact that I was already over an hour late for my first day at the comprehensive from hell.

We eventually arrived at Dylan's school. I waited in the car. Mum was gone for ages. I could hear Dylan's screams from the car park! When Mum finally emerged she looked dishevelled to say the least! We didn't speak for a while, as she was obviously as traumatised by the incident as Dylan had been. I was quietly feeling more and more nauseous. When we pulled up outside the school gates I was ready to pass out. Even though Mum was late herself, she insisted on taking me in. I didn't say so, but I was grateful. If she hadn't, I'm convinced my jelly-like legs would have gone from under me. I had really bad vibes about the day, and I wasn't wrong.

We eventually found our way to the head teacher's office. He wasn't very impressed with us for being late, but Mum did her best impression of a dizzy blonde. At first I was really embarrassed and annoyed – she was acting as though Women's Lib had never happened! But on the other hand, watching her use her feminine charm was amazing! She had Mr Blanchard wrapped round her finger in seconds and he was agreeing that the city's one-way system is terrible and was trying to talk Mum into joining an evening class for basic motor mechanics! Then he offered to show me to my new class personally. I said bye to Mum and she blew me a kiss. At least, I think it was meant for me. Come to think of it, Mr Blanchard did have a smile on his face and a spring in his step afterwards!

Then I had to face the ordeal of meeting my new teacher – and a new class. I was shaking like a leaf when I went in. I could feel every eye in the room on me. I felt as though I was walking to my seat in slow motion. I just wanted the floor to open up and swallow me whole! Eventually, I felt brave enough to look around. I avoided eye contact with anyone, until I noticed a girl grinning at me! I was a bit freaked out, but at the end of the lesson she introduced herself and her friend as Nina and Rachael. (Hey! I've managed to remember their names!) They both seemed really friendly and even invited me to spend the lunch hour with them! I could've hugged them (but controlled myself!). I spent the rest of the day following them round like a lost puppy. I couldn't even go to the loo on my own! I felt so vulnerable! Thank god for these angels of mercy!

Still, it was a tough day. I felt like I had two heads, judging by the strange looks I got. You'd think they'd never seen a girl wearing love beads and army boots, with black eyeliner, and talking with an unusual accent before! This is supposed to be the big city! I can see I'm going to have my work cut out educating them in the ways of Jasmine Fields. They won't know what's hit them!

Tuesday, Sept. 14th, 7.00 p.m.

Hooray! Another day over with! I actually managed to get more than three hours' sleep at last, but I still looked rough this morning. Getting the bus was pretty bad too. There were thousands of kids fighting for seats. It was mad! And I didn't have to worry about keeping an eye out for my stop either. I was dragged along in the general direction of school in the sea of lime-green uniforms!

I'd worked out a plan of action – to track down Nina and Rachael as quickly as possible and cling on to them for dear life! I thought it would be like finding a needle in a haystack, but they were waiting for me at the gates! I've been so lucky! They are really kind. OK, I'll be honest. Under different circumstances I'd be bored to tears by them, but I'm not. I'm just grateful that I'm not on my own in that hell-hole!

Wednesday, Sept. 15th, 4.30 p.m.

I've never felt so ridiculous! I'm embarrassed just writing about it! It's my own fault. I should've waited before making a break for independence. Nina and Rachael told me I'd get lost, but their condescending tone got too much for me. Actually, I found my way to the loos easily – and completely unchaperoned!

But how was I to know the bell would go while I was still in there? I didn't have a clue where to go! I was completely lost in a crowd of thousands. When panic set in and I asked a friendly face for help, I was totally ignored! Either he was unable to understand my accent or was frightened by my manic expression, but he just left me there. Seconds later, the corridor was empty and I was on my own and on the verge of hysteria! I couldn't believe my luck when this little Year Seven boy appeared from nowhere. I swallowed my pride and asked him for help. Thankfully, he took pity on me and by a strange twist of fate, knew exactly where I should be. (His sister Bryony is in my class, apparently.) He even insisted on escorting me right to the door and explaining to my teacher what had happened. I felt so stupid! Everyone was laughing at me, and when my little hero waved through the window there was uproar! The whole class erupted into peals of laughter and a girl, who I presumed was his sister, said she'd arrange a date for us if I was interested! I was so humiliated! I've never felt so stupid in all my life! So now everyone will think I'm a total loser. What can I do to convince them that I'm not? I certainly feel like one right now.

Thursday, Sept. 16th, 8.40 p.m.

Only one more day to go and I've finished a whole week. I can't wait for the weekend. Poppy's offered to help me choose a colour scheme for my room. I think she's looking forward to putting her artistic skills to good use. Mum won't let her loose anywhere else!

Friday, Sept. 17th, 6.00 p.m.

HOORAY! The weekend starts here! I can't believe I've survived the week! I am exhausted! I've only got a bit of homework to do, so I can get stuck into this room. Nina and Rachael invited me to join them at chess club tomorrow morning. Chess club? On a Saturday morning? No thank you! I'm sorry, but I'd rather have a lie in – or at least try. I'd rather sit with Poppy and watch Brad's paint dry even! I'm afraid to say it, but my new friends are quite definitely nerds. They are lovely people, but I just can't dig them, man! I need to find someone on my wavelength before I go mad!

I miss Carmel. Mum said I can ring her over the weekend, but I'm really nervous. I might leave it until tomorrow when I've finished my homework. Then I can try to relax a bit and be more like my old self! She wouldn't recognise me now. I've become a hermit, a cradle-snatcher, an embarrassment and almost a member of a chess club! How could I possibly expect her to treat me normally? I'm not normal any more! I'm trying to fit in, and failing miserably!

Saturday, Sept. 18th, 7.00 p.m.

What would I normally be doing on a Saturday night? Going to the cinema, for a pizza, maybe even some bowling or skating in town. I certainly wouldn't be sitting in front of the TV, eating a box of chocolates for comfort food and writing in my diary! I'd have a social life! Maybe I should've joined the chess club. God! How desperate am I? I'm ringing Carmel. Maybe she can save me!

8.30 p.m.

I knew I'd feel strange once I'd spoken to Carmel. I can't really describe *how* I feel though. It's weird. She still sounded the same (of course) and was excited to hear from me. And although I felt quite sad talking to her at first, she did cheer me up eventually. Like she said, she's only a phonecall away, and we'll be seeing each other every school holiday. She's right. Just because I'm far away, it doesn't mean I can't be part of their lives any more. It just means I'm going to have to rely on her to fill me in with all the scandal and gossip! It won't be quite as exciting as seeing it all with my own eyes, but Carmel makes things sound funnier than they really are anyway!

She told me how much everyone was missing me, and that they all send their love. Then she made me feel guilty about not ringing sooner! Now I know it's not going to be difficult or depressing speaking to her, I might start ringing more often. That's if Mum agrees to me using the phone more, of course! We did talk for rather a long time! I don't think Mum minded too much this time, but I doubt she'll be as understanding once the bills start rolling in . . .

Sunday, Sept. 19th, 5.40 p.m.

What a luxury! Shops that open on a Sunday! We walked round for ages getting utterly lost. I don't think we managed to see even half of the town centre either. And everyone here is so trendy! They all looked ready for a night out!

We traipsed round loads of DIY stores for hours. Poppy thinks she knows all there is to know about colour schemes now. Just because she starts art college next week and has got a hot date with Brad! (I think her rampant hormones might have had something to do with Mum's decision to hire him!) She thinks my taste in interior design leaves a lot to be desired. She said the colours I've chosen will probably induce migraines. I don't care! As long as they make me feel bright and cheerful. I feel like I need cheering up a bit today.

9.00 p.m.

Wow! I definitely think Dad and I have some kind of psychic connection. He rang me just as I was about to ring him! Weird! I told him all about my week. He reassured me that it's bound to take us a while to settle in, but convinced me that in a few weeks I'll be Ms Popular again. He sounded a bit happier tonight too. Kay's had another ultrasound scan. They don't want to know the sex. I'm glad. I want a surprise too. I still haven't decided if I'd prefer another brother or sister. I suppose that's quite good really, considering I'll be practically a stranger anyway! Oh. I promised I'd think positive! Snap out of it, Jaz!

Monday, Sept. 20th, 7.10 p.m.

To say I felt a bit more relaxed in school today would be exaggerating. But I did feel less anxious than last week. I recognised two rooms and three teachers today! I was quite proud of myself. I am also starting to recognise a few more faces too, although I don't know many names yet. I see one girl from my class on the bus in the morning. She gave me half of a 'don't I know you?' smile this morning. I think she must've momentarily forgotten that I was the new kid who hangs round with the chess-playing nerds.

Oh. I'm horrible. Nina and Rachael are very . . . what's the word? . . . inoffensive, but if I don't make a break for it soon, I'll be stuck with them. Much as I'm grateful to them, that'd be a fate worse than death! I'm permanently on my best behaviour just in case my strange ways freak them out! I simply can't be myself or relax around them like I can with Carmel and the gang back home. And on top of that, they are definitely easy targets for bullies. I'm sure I heard that Bryony girl asking Nina if she could borrow her homework to check the answers! The cheek of her!

Even worse, Bryony must've noticed me earwigging. She pointed me out to this older boy and introduced me as 'the hippy girl who stole little Clarke's heart!' (I presume Clarke is her brother – the Year Seven kid who rescued me – and embarrassed me horrendously. I still haven't lived that down!)

I should've just ignored her. But, typical me, before I could stop myself, my mouth took on a life of its own and I answered, 'I'm no cradle-snatcher. I prefer more mature men myself!'

The boy with her burst out laughing and said, 'Watch out, Bry. You might have some competition on your hands now!' and winked at me! 'Bry' was obviously not amused. She gave me a look that could kill and stormed off!

I was shaking a bit from the adrenaline afterwards. I'm going to have to watch my mouth with her. She's obviously the coolest girl in the school. She can even manage to make the uniform look good! Her hair is just perfect and her make-up is immaculate. No wonder she's got this gorgeous boyfriend! Judging by the gang of girls she's always got round her, she's the one I've got to get in with if I want to make friends. But what chance have I got now? She thinks I was flirting with her boyfriend! I probably just made myself her mortal enemy or, worse still, a social outcast! Maybe I should start learning the rules of chess after all . . .

Tuesday, Sept. 21st, 6.10 p.m.

I spent all night worrying about what was going to happen with Bryony today. Maybe I needn't have bothered. This fitting in lark is a piece of cake! The girl at the bus stop smiled at me this morning! I grabbed the chance to make conversation. I asked whether or not Bryony had put a death-warrant on my head. She laughed and told me Bryony's bark is worse than her bite and that I'd probably done the best thing a new kid could, and stood up to her. Apparently she already had me down as another easy target! At least she's not going to bully me, but will she bother giving me the time of day?

Wednesday, Sept. 22nd, 10.00 p.m.

I kept my distance from Bryony again today, to give her a chance to cool down. She is just so sophisticated! I heard her describing a cocktail dress she had to wear to go to some party with Richard. That must be her boyfriend! How cool is that? Everyone was hanging on her every word – she is definitely the ringleader of the cool crowd.

I've decided. I've got to be part of that. I can't risk being a loser here. It's hard enough already just being the new kid, the one with the funny accent and weird boots. There's no way I'm going to spend the next five years looking over my shoulder and worrying about who's going to walk all over me next. I want an easy life! I just want to get on with my work and do well without getting hassled. I'm going to have to get round Bryony somehow. Just one problem – how?

Thursday, Sept. 23rd, 9.50 p.m.

Never again will I doubt the existence of fate! We were in the Chemistry lab when Bryony came in late. She was obviously unimpressed when Dr Monkman made her sit next to me! She gave me a seriously dirty look, and spent half of the lesson leaning across me to talk to her friends.

We were given some insultingly simple experiments to do. I was so bored, but then I noticed there were all the right ingredients to make a stink bomb! Either I could be a lifelong honorary member of the local chess club, or I could impress the coolest girl in the school by getting us the afternoon off! (The possibility of being expelled from school before I'd completed a whole term didn't occur to me!) Before my conscience had a chance to convince me otherwise, I was mixing.

Then I realised what I'd done! Within seconds the horrendous stench was filling the room. Dr Monkman looked more like a madman, tearing round the lab like one possessed! It didn't take him long to locate the source. I almost died when he went directly to Bryony and started to accuse her. I was as good as dead! There was nothing else to do but interrupt him. I did an impression of a stupid new girl that would've made Mum proud! I told him not to blame her but me, and it had been an accident. His face went so red that I thought he would explode! He told everyone else to take a study break in the library and asked me and Bryony to wait.

Nina and Rachael looked horrified! I felt so ashamed. I sat there, shaking. I was more worried about Bryony's reaction than Dr Monkman's! She didn't say a word, just scowled at me while I apologised. I told her I'd take full responsibility to which she just said, 'You'd better'. When he came over, he quietly apologised to her and told her she could go. That's when I realised how stupid I'd been! My stomach was in such a knot. I thought I was going to be sick! He was furious and gave me a lecture on safety in the lab and said that he wouldn't tolerate irresponsible and dangerous behaviour. I was waiting for him to send me to Mr Blanchard's office, but instead he told me he'd read my glowing report from my last school, and would put this down to an accident! He gave me detention tomorrow, a two hundred word essay to write on the rules of appropriate laboratory behaviour and a warning there'll be no second chances. One step out of line, and I'll be out before I can say sulphuric acid!

All the way home, I was actually considering not telling Mum. She'd never find out, because she'd still be in work while I was in detention. But Poppy would want to know why I was late. She knows I've got no friends so I couldn't make up a reasonable excuse. Mum would find out sooner or later, so I told her. She went berserk and that was after I'd toned it down and given her the accident storyline too! She gave me a lecture on irresponsibility and how I should be trying especially hard to create a good impression and fit in! I could hardly tell her that was exactly what I *was* doing! She said she wouldn't bother telling Dad because it would worry him unnecessarily, but I'm more concerned about what Bryony's reaction is going to be tomorrow!

Friday, Sept. 24th, 12.30 p.m.

How sad am I? There I am doing all these stupid things in the vain hope of impressing someone, when all I've managed to do is make myself completely friendless. Nina and Rachael have been avoiding me all day. They weren't even waiting for me at the gates this morning. Now here I am, writing in my diary during lunch break just to look like I'm doing something, rather than looking like a total loser here on my own.

8.00 p.m.

Hoorah! It's not all terrible! As I was leaving detention, I saw the girl from the bus stop. She came right over and said thanks and that it was the funniest Chemistry lesson they'd ever had! Wow! How great is that? I asked her if Bryony wasn't too annoyed about being blamed for it. She told me to keep out of her way for a few more days, but she must've thought it pretty cool herself, otherwise I'd have known about it by now! Maybe it wasn't such a disaster after all. Perhaps my plan did work!

But on the downside, I experienced a detention for the first time in my entire life! It was awful. Some of the kids there were pretty scary! I certainly don't intend doing it ever again, that's for sure!

Sunday, Sept. 26th, 7.50 p.m.

Another fun-filled weekend *chez* Fields. I had more lectures from Mum, so I rang Dad to hear a friendly voice. Then I filled Carmel in with all the gory details. She definitely thinks I'm cracking up. Maybe I am. She did make me realise how stupid I'd been. I could've been suspended or worse! We did laugh about it though, eventually.

Monday, Sept. 27th, 9.00 p.m.

I'm sick of Mum working late every night. Poppy's out with her new art student friends and Dylan is having another sleepover! He's got a better social life than I have, and more friends! Nina and Rachael are only just speaking to me. I think they think I'm a bit wild! Mind you, they're not the only ones, according to Bryony's boyfriend. I almost died when he tapped me on the shoulder in the canteen. I am a legend! The news even reached his year group and they were impressed! Bryony wasn't. She said it was childish and her clothes still smelled.

Tuesday, Sept. 28th, 6.20 p.m.

Oh god. Had another run-in with Bryony today. Rachael complimented me in art class about how good the tie-dyed T-shirt I'd made was. Bryony butted in and said, 'She's got an unfair advantage. With a name like Jasmine Fields she probably wore tie-dyed nappies on a hippie commune!'

Everyone was laughing at me! It was horrible. I should've just ignored her, but of course I couldn't and retorted that I hadn't lived on a commune, just been conceived on one! Everyone laughed except Bryony. She just gave me a sarcastic grin. Better than a smack, I suppose, but I think I've got a way to go before I can win her round!

OCTOBER

Friday, Oct. 1st, 8.50 p.m.

Oh, I can't wait for the day that I actually enjoy Friday evenings again! All I've got to look forward to is going to a flea market with Poppy tomorrow morning. She reckons we can get loads of cool stuff for my room there. Actually, it looks pretty good already. Even Mum is impressed. She bought me a lovely potted palm as a little thank-you for doing so much around the house, for helping with Dylan, for putting up with Poppy and Brad snogging all the time (they've only been together a matter of days and they're already joined at the hip – or even lip!), and for trying so hard to fit in. She's right. I have tried hard. I am still trying. I wonder if I will ever need to stop trying?

Saturday, Oct. 2nd, 4.50 p.m.

I felt like a right gooseberry today at the flea market with Poppy and Brad. He couldn't keep his hands off her! It was so embarrassing! I left them alone and was up to my armpits in a bin-bag full of smelly old clothes, when I looked up to see Bryony with her boyfriend! Of all the times and places! I must've looked ridiculous! I was standing there holding a moth-eaten old T-shirt in one hand and some strange backscratching device in the other!

Bryony was so obviously enjoying my embarrassment! Her boyfriend said hello and a woman behind me answered him! It was his mum! I'd been scavenging through her stall! I had hold of one of his old T-shirts! *Eek!* At least it wasn't his underpants!

Monday, Oct. 4th, 6.10 p.m.

Argh! We've got an assignment to do! I thought Mrs Wallis was joking when she put me with Bryony, but apparently her name is Foster and we were put in pairs alphabetically. What a bizarre twist of fate!

We've got to work together for two weeks! Part of me is terrified, but part of me thinks it's great – it's my big chance to impress her!

I was expecting Bryony to say something catty about my wonderful impression of a bag lady in the flea market, but she didn't. At least, I didn't hear her telling everyone. That's not to say she didn't tell them. Well. Now I've got a chance to show her that I'm not a loser. We'll get an 'A' for this project, even if it kills me!

Tuesday, Oct. 5th, 4.30 p.m.

Bryony suggested that we meet in the canteen lunchtime to discuss the project – then she kept me waiting for ten minutes! When she finally turned up, she didn't even apologise for being late. I could have been annoyed if I'd thought about it, but I decided to show my mature side – I calmly took out a notebook and pen and we jotted down a few ideas. She said she wanted to do well and hoped I was going to take it as seriously as her. I think so! I need to impress both her and Mrs Wallis, so this is my chance to kill two birds with one stone!

Wednesday, Oct. 6th, 6.00 p.m.

I think I must be getting round Bryony at last! She keeps smiling and asking if I'm OK. She even let me sit near them today in Maths. I was hoping to do the same at lunch, but I had to go to the library. I bumped into Nina and Rachael there. They told me not to trust Bryony, but I think they're just jealous.

Thursday, Oct. 7th, 10.30 p.m.

I joined our local library tonight. It's so cool! The place is huge and I was utterly spoiled for choice! I got a load more books. I'll take them in to show Bryony tomorrow. I wonder how she's been getting on?

Friday, Oct. 8th, 6.00 p.m.

My back is killing me! After me dragging in half a Brazilian rainforest's worth of books, Bryony found about five minutes to glance at them. I suppose it's my own fault for interrupting her during break. She told me that she wouldn't have any time over the weekend to do any reading, because Richard's just got a new car and is taking her out! Wow! He's so much older than she is! Her parents must be as cool as she is. Mine would kill me if I told them I had a seventeen-year-old boyfriend! (I should be so lucky! Saying that, I'm not bothered about boyfriends, just any friend would do me at the moment!) So I'm going to have a busy weekend after all. I suppose I should be grateful really. At least it'll give me something to do!

Sunday, Oct. 10th, 3.25 p.m.

I've hardly left my room all weekend, give or take a ten-second break to speak to Dad. After spending so much time in here, I have to admit that Poppy had a point. The décor does tend to give you eyestrain after a while! Either that or it's all the reading I've done. Mum said she's considering going into school to complain about the amount of homework we get. I could hardly tell her that this project is supposed to be a team effort, but my other team member is too busy enjoying herself to help! I have been working flat out, but I want to do well. It's hard being the new kid.

Monday, Oct. 11th, 5.10 p.m.

I can't believe it! I asked Bryony what kind of weekend she'd had and apparently Richard's car hadn't arrived, so they had a quiet weekend at home! I've worked myself into the ground while she's done absolutely nothing! Then she said that she had no way to get in touch with me so I gave her my address and she even made a sarcastic comment about that! She read it and asked if I had a silver spoon in my mouth. I told her the best I had was a few amalgam fillings! Richard burst out laughing, but I don't think Bryony appreciated my sense of humour! Or, more likely, she doesn't like anyone else getting the last word. But when I suggested we meet up this week, she did agree. She suggested coming to see the mansion I live in! I wasn't very keen on the idea at first, but it could be OK. Maybe I could do something to eat for us both. It might just work out yet.

Tuesday, Oct. 12th, 4.50 p.m.

Bryony actually walked with me to Biology today! I felt great walking along with the cool crowd! Nina looked surprised when she saw me. I felt so embarrassed for her when she dropped her bag and its contents all over the floor! Bryony and the gang started laughing. I know I should've gone to help. Instead I just stood back and watched her frantically scrabbling around for everything. I still feel terrible. I'm not sure if becoming Bryony's friend is the solution to all my problems after all. Not if it means I'm going to have to behave like that all the time.

Wednesday, Oct. 13th, 10.00 p.m.

Well. I'm glad Mum wasn't here when my visitor arrived. She's been making such a fuss about meeting my new friend Bryony that she'd have been disappointed with a ten-minute visit! I know I was! I'd gone to all the hassle of making sandwiches and Mum had even made her special chocolate cake. Still, thinking positively now, that means all the more for me later! All we'd managed to do was read some of my notes before Bryony started on about the other things she should be doing. She made me feel really guilty for keeping her when she told me all about her friend Kate who lives just round the corner. She's been off school for ages with glandular fever and has only just started feeling well enough to have visitors. I felt lousy stopping Bryony from seeing her sick friend, so I went through everything in record speed. But I've ended up doing most of the talking, most of the writing and now the rewriting too. I'm not very impressed at all, really. Still, Bryony's promised to type it all up, which is something, I suppose.

Thursday, Oct. 14th, 10.10 p.m.

Hooray! Finally it's finished! I gave Bryony all the notes today, so I am now doing my best impression of a couch potato! I just hope I can trust her to have it finished for tomorrow.

Friday, Oct. 15th, 4.30 p.m.

I can't believe it! I knew the assignment looked really professional, but I never imagined that it actually was! No wonder Bryony offered to do it when her sister is a secretary. She did all the work for her! I can't say anything either, because I don't want to land Richard in trouble for telling me. His poor face was a picture when he realised I didn't know! I'm so mad! I did all that work and she couldn't even type it up herself. I'm really losing patience with this sucking-up-to-Bryony business. She may be cool, but frankly she's a manipulative cow and I don't think I want to put up with being treated like this any more!

Saturday, Oct. 16th, 2.00 p.m.

I told Carmel about the assignment fiasco. She told me not to lose sleep over it. In fact, she said it wasn't like me to be so stressed out. She's right. I am stressed! My whole life is stressful now. Nothing's straightforward any more. I rang Carmel to cheer myself up, but now I'm depressed. She's such a good friend and I really miss her, but I've realised I've hardly given her or Dad a second thought these past few days. I've been so busy and preoccupied with school – and now I feel guilty. Maybe without me noticing, I am starting to settle in here after all – in some fashion. But I don't want to forget everyone! And also I don't want to miss out. I'm not really a part of things at home any more. Carmel told me she'd seen Dad and Kay. Apparently, her bump is starting to show now. I can't believe my best friend sees more of my dad than I do. Worse still though, she'll see my new brother or sister grow up and I won't.

Sunday, Oct. 17th, 3.30 p.m.

I had a row with Mum this morning. She told me I should be out enjoying myself at weekends with my friends! The fact is, I agree! That's what makes it so ridiculous! We were arguing over something we both agree on! When she suggested that I call my friend Bryony and go out with her it made me feel even worse! I wish I could, but she obviously didn't want me to have her number, otherwise she would have given it to me when I gave her mine. I think that says it all, really. I've still got a long way to go. I just want to have a life again.

Monday, Oct. 18th, 6.40 p.m.

Poppy walked me to the bus stop. Both her and Mum are worried about me. I told her I'm worried too! I've become a totally different person since I came here! I'm more like a recluse every day!

The rest of my family, on the other hand, are acting like they've been here for ever! Poppy is having a whale of a time in art college and she and the gorgeous Brad seem to be getting serious. Dylan thinks this is the best adventure he's ever had and seems to be the most popular boy in the school, judging by the number of birthday parties he's invited to! Mum is revelling in her new job, works like a dog and loves every minute of it, and looks twice as glamorous and happy as she ever did before. Poppy reckons there is a man at work who is keen on her! I wouldn't be surprised! She looks great! But what's wrong with me then? Why are things easy for everyone else and not me? I'm going to have to do something about it! Maybe join some after school clubs or something. I know! T'ai chi! I need better karma and inner peace! This city life is hard work. Yes. That's the answer. I need to chill out!

Tuesday, Oct. 19th, 10.30 p.m.

Hooray! A- for my first assignment! I'm so pleased! And, as if that wasn't good enough, Mrs Wallis made me and Bryony stand up in front of the class. She told everyone it was an excellent team effort. (Little did she know!) Then we had to answer loads of questions about it, and that was the most satisfying bit by far. I actually felt a bit sorry for Bryony – she must've felt stupid – she could hardly answer anything! In fact, I looked like a genius next to her! (Which, of course, I am!) I couldn't have planned things any better! Revenge is sweet – or should that be justice? Anyway, I've decided to go with the flow from now on. If something's meant to be, fate will sort it out.

Friday, Oct. 22nd, 6.30 p.m.

Very uneventful couple of days – and now we've got a week off! I can't believe it's half term already – we've been here for nearly two months! It's gone so quickly – in some ways.

I also can't believe that Dad has got a conference in Brighton in *this* week of all weeks! He's taking Kay with him for a week by the sea, so I can't go and stay with them and see everyone. Lucky Carmel has gone for a week's holiday, so I can't even go and stay with her family. It's such a pain! A week of no friends – just taking Dylan down the park, or wandering round the town *on my own*. Oh, *what* fun!

Wednesday, Oct. 27th, 11.30 a.m.

Bored! Bored, bored, bored. Yes, I've read some *brilliant* books. And I've got to know our corner of the city a bit (not very exciting). But there's only so much reading and walking and watching crap TV a girl can do!! I miss my old friends! I want some fun! It's so bad – I'm even looking forward to going back to school!! I've done *all* my homework already – it's so sad. Ah well, Mum's taken pity on me and has promised to leave work at a decent time tonight and go out for dinner. It's the closest thing to a social life I've had this week . . .

Sunday, Oct. 31st, 10.00 p.m.

Yes!! School! People my own age! Potential friends! I'm going to crack this. I have a good vibe. I'm determined to be settled and happy by Christmas!

I have had one laugh this week, though – seeing Dylan and all his little friends dressed up for Hallowe'en. He looked so cute! (I wish I'd had an invitation to a party.)

Today is the only day in the year that I don't get funny looks because of the way I'm dressed!

NOVEMBER

Monday, Nov. 1st, 10.00 p.m.

I think it cheered Mum up seeing me so happy setting off for school. I must admit, I felt more of a spring in my step than was usual! It didn't last long though. I got all depressed when I heard a girl laughing – she sounded exactly the same as Carmel! For a second I thought it actually was her, but then I remembered!

I heard the laugh again later, too. It was this tiny girl with bright orange curly hair. I hadn't seen her before. The whole class gathered round her like she was a famous pop star or some kind of celebrity! Even Ms Green joined the crowd. I heard her say, 'Welcome back, Kate.' Bryony's friend Kate? Surely not! I can't see it myself. She doesn't look sophisticated enough for Bryony to hang out with! Her clothes aren't cool and her hair isn't trendy and, more importantly, she's amazingly popular! I hardly know Bryony at all, but I'd say Kate is the type of person Bryony would be jealous of!

Tuesday, Nov. 2nd, 4.50 p.m.

The world-famous Jasmine Fields gut reaction was right again! I was people-watching in the canteen when I spotted Kate. She ran over and flung her little arms round Richard's neck. Bryony's body language told me straight away that she wasn't pleased! She was so bitchy! 'Good god, Katie! That glandular fever was a blessing in disguise! You've lost some of your puppy fat at last!' I'd have smacked her if that were me. (Well, maybe not!) I felt like cheering when Kate answered her back, 'Well, I'd much rather be a chubby pup than a skinny old dog, any day!' I burst out laughing! I couldn't stop myself! It must've been obvious I was earwigging. Bryony gave me a filthy look, but I still couldn't stop! In fact, I was still chuckling when Kate came over. I thought she was going to say something about me minding my own business, but instead she asked if she could sit with me. She hates eating alone apparently. I'm sure she could've had her pick of people to sit with, but I'm not complaining! I was a bit nervous at first, but we chatted all lunch. She seems really nice actually. Now I know why everyone is so happy to have her back, and why Bryony isn't!

Wednesday, Nov. 3rd, 5.00 p.m.

Yesss! At last! I have finally had a proper conversation. The real Jasmine is back and it feels great! Kate is so friendly. I asked if she was OK because she looked really tired today. She told me that she still feels wiped out – glandular fever sounds awful. She hardly left the house for months! Poor thing. She said she's never been so bored in her whole life and that she was actually looking forward to coming back to school! I could certainly understand how she felt!

I wasn't sure if she was joking when she said that she'd even missed Bryony. I was so relieved when she apologised for being sarcastic. I knew they'd never be friends! She asked if 'Bryony the bitch' was making my life a misery yet. I gave her a quick run-down of some of the things she's done so far. I couldn't believe it when Kate said Bryony'd been just as mean to her when she first came here. She told me that I've just got to stand up to her and not let her get to me. If only it were that easy.

I was really surprised when I looked at my watch. We'd been chatting for ages! She's so easy to talk to. When she asked me about my pendant, she got my whole life story! I must've talked for ages, but the best thing was, she actually seemed interested.

7.10 p.m.

I've just been to explore the local leisure centre with Poppy. It's amazing! It is so big! There are literally thousands of things going on. It was hard to choose, but I'm sticking with t'ai chi classes. I'm not especially looking forward to going alone, but like Mum said, maybe I'll make some friends! God knows I need to!

Friday, Nov. 5th, 6.30 p.m.

Hooray! This is just so great! I have been invited to a firework display! I can't believe it! I think Mum was pleasantly surprised too. I thought she was going to cry! I could've cried myself when Kate asked me. Who cares if Bryony wasn't too keen? I'm going to be like Kate. She doesn't give two hoots about what Bryony thinks, so neither will I! Oh god! I'm wasting precious clothes-picking time. What am I going to wear?!!

Saturday, Nov. 6th, 10.00 a.m.

Phew! I've forgotten how tiring having a social life is! I'm shattered and I've got to go shopping with Mum, too. Still, at least she's promised to buy me something from the shop Kate pointed out to me last night on our way out. It looked fantastic – full to the brim of joss-sticks, love beads and amazing tie-dye and batik outfits! Maybe she will treat me to some more clothes which 'express my Geminian personality'! I much prefer that to 'hippy chick', which Bryony keeps calling me. She's just so square when it comes to clothes! I think I totally freaked her out when I called her 'a typically conservative, fashion-conscious Virgo'. I must've hit the nail on the head judging by her reaction and when I told her that guessing star signs is a skill of us white witches, she soon shut up! Maybe I could put a spell on her if she carries on being nasty!

The evening was really different to what I expected. I was all set to go straight home after the fireworks. I've obviously got a long way to go before I'm as cool as the others are! The night had only just started for them! They hung around in a carpark snogging each other, being loud and some were even smoking and drinking! I'm glad I went, but I ended up feeling like an immature impostor and a real bore! They are way out of my league. Not that I'm really sure I want to be in that league.

But the big surprise of the evening was when Richard offered me a lift home. I think Bryony was surprised too! She must've had other ideas, but he insisted. I felt like I was breaking up the party a bit, but he said he had to pick up his little brother

Saul anyway. Bryony didn't miss that one. Another opportunity to publicly humiliate me about my little 'liaison' with her brother Clarke. Thankfully, Richard soon shut her up. And I thought she was the queen of dirty looks! She must've learned all she knew from him! He's so nice. I wonder why he's with her?

But guess what? His little brother is even nicer still! In fact, I'm worried that Bryony might be right about my cradle-snatching urges! So what if he is in the year below me? He's gorgeous!

Monday, Nov. 8th, 10.00 p.m.

Whooh! My life is just too weird sometimes! Having missed the bus, been late to pick up Dylan from school, and then been caught in a downpour on the way home, I could hardly be bothered to go to the leisure centre. I told Poppy I was tired, which was true, but I was also terrified of going on my own! She ended up dragging me along with her because she's joined the gym with Brad! She really must be serious about him! Poppy pumping iron – I don't think so!

Anyway, t'ai chi was scary, but really good, and I

was starting to get the hang of it too (at about the same time as the lesson ended!). But walking home provided the most exciting moment of my time here yet! After all, it's not every day the man (OK, boy) of your dreams knocks you over on his skateboard! Ahh! Romance! I was quite literally swept off my feet! I still can't believe it was him. Of all the people to nearly concuss me it was him. Saul. *Phwoar!*

Thank god I was so laid-back after the lesson. Public humiliation on such a grand scale at any other time would've meant instant death to the culprit! It must've been divine intervention. It's too much of a coincidence for it not to be. I thought I'd died and gone to heaven when I rolled over and looked into his blue eyes! (I suppose his eyes were open so wide in shock. After all, I suppose I could've actually died!) And he was so apologetic too! And so kind. He even helped dust me down! *Phwoar!* He is gorgeous! I'm still blushing remembering it! I actually thought he was going to kiss me at one point. The way he leaned right over me! I couldn't breathe! But he must've realised he was staring and backed off. He told me he'd been admiring my pendant. Apparently, he's really into stones and mine is a beauty!

If Poppy hadn't come out then, who knows what might've happened. I mean, her timing couldn't have been worse! And she embarrassed me horribly. She'd heard everything. Poor Saul went bright red when she said she'd not heard that chat-up line before. I could've killed her! He apologised again, and quickly skated off. Poppy still hasn't stopped laughing about it. I'll get her back. It's her birthday a week on Wednesday. Maybe I could think of something equally embarrassing for then.

Tuesday, Nov. 9th, 9.45 p.m.

I was telling Kate about my t'ai chi lesson today and I ended up telling her about Saul too! I was a bit nervous – worrying that she'd laugh at me for cradle-snatching, like Bryony does – but she so cool! She knows him too and said she's never seen a dreamier boy ever! I agreed. How great is this? Not only does Kate appreciate my bizarre hobbies, eccentric sense of humour and my decorated DMs, but she fancies the same boys as me! Amazing! We were just obviously meant to be friends.

We had a great laugh talking about it, but I still swore her to total secrecy. I dread to think what Bryony's reaction would be if she knew. Her gang all go out with seventeen-year-olds! My life would be over if Kate said anything. I'd be the uncoolest, weirdest kid in the school. Hold on. What's wrong with me? I already am!

The second cool thing today was that I got revenge on Poppy for being so wicked to Saul! I asked Brad what he had planned for her birthday present. When he said a necklace, I suggested something less boring and I thought that maybe he should have a rethink. Oh! I'm so cruel, but I couldn't help myself. I told him she loved cuddly toys, especially pink ones! I sensed he wasn't sure, but hopefully I convinced him. After all, little sister knows best! With a bit of luck, he'll get one with ribbons all over it too. She's bound to love that – not!

Wednesday, Nov. 17th, 9.10 p.m.

Dad rang. He wanted to wish Poppy happy birthday but she'd gone out for a romantic meal with Brad. (I wonder if she appreciated her present?) Anyway, it gave me more time to chat to him. I asked after Kay. He said she's getting tired a lot now, but looking forward to having a rest over Christmas. Christmas! I can't believe it's coming round so fast! Dad was asking about our plans. I suppose he needs to know so he can make his own. God! I can't even start to think about it. And I'm sure I won't need to. After all, I'm still a child and not able to make my own decisions, as Mum keeps reminding me. I'll leave it to them to fight it out.

Thursday, Nov. 18th, 9.50 p.m.

God. I'm getting sick of this place. For once, I'm not even talking about school either. Poppy went mad with me! Brad had got her a fluffy pink rabbit and a balloon! Brilliant! She must've been mortified! Serves her right for embarrassing me and Saul like that. She thinks she's so grown up now she's in college.

As for Mum! She's driving me mad! I mention Christmas and she flies right off the handle. So now I'm left in limbo! What are we going to do? Working out Christmas Day timetables in the past was always hard enough. That was in the good old days when there was only a few minutes' drive between our house and Dad's. Now there's hours. I can see what's coming – a miserable Christmas. Someone's bound to end up unhappy. Or, should I say, unhappier.

Tuesday, Nov. 23rd, 10.00 p.m.

I am *so* tired! If the teachers give us any more home-work I think I'll expire!!

Friday, Nov. 26th, 4.10 p.m.

I don't believe this. I've been invited to a girls' night at Kate's house tonight – how totally brilliant? But I get home and Mum says I can't go. I know she wants me to go out with the family for Poppy's birthday, (now Poppy and I are talking again! I eventually got her and Brad to see the funny side!) and I want to go with them, but her birthday's already gone so what difference would waiting another night make? We could go tomorrow night instead. Poppy said she doesn't mind, and it's her birthday celebration, so why won't Mum cut me some slack? It's always the same. We have to fit in with her busy lifestyle, but she can't make allowances for us! Now I've got to go and play happy families instead of making friends, and this was such a huge breakthrough for me! It's so unfair!

Saturday, Nov. 27th, 11.10 a.m.

What a night! No wonder Mum made a big fuss about me going. She's got a boyfriend! And she had the nerve to invite him along for the meal! Doesn't she have a clue? He seems OK and everything, but bringing him last night! It was hardly the appropriate time or place to meet my possible future stepdad! I thought Poppy and Brad were annoying, but watching Mum giggling like a teenager was enough to put me off my moussaka. Thank god I had Dylan there to keep me occupied. I'd have died of boredom otherwise! God. That's a bad sign. I'm appreciating Dylan's company! I've got to get a life! But then I could've been doing exactly that round at Kate's. I bet they had a great time. Honestly. My life is like a badly-written sitcom sometimes! No one would ever believe it if I told them!

Sunday, Nov. 28th, 3.15 p.m.

Mum and 'James' are taking Dylan bowling tonight. They did invite me, but I feel like doing my moody teenager routine. Actually, I've got a stack of homework to do, but if she thinks I'm going to welcome 'Uncle Jimmy' into the fold that quickly, she's sadly mistaken. (I'm a teenager. It's my job to be awkward!)

Monday, Nov. 29th, 6.30 p.m.

Argh! I am *so* mad! Thank goodness I've got t'ai chi soon. I need calming down! I just knew I'd miss an excellent night at Kate's house. It would've been great. I'm so angry with Mum! We're not getting on at all at the moment. She just hasn't got a clue how hard this is for me. She thinks I'm down on James.

I'm not. I'm just annoyed with her for making me miss a good night at Kate's!

Then I had to listen to another lecture. This time it was about how I should give her a break, that she knows it's not easy, but this is her first relationship since Dad. She forgets that I know all this! I've been trying to get her to go out with someone for ages. Until we moved, it was one of my hobbies! It's about time she met someone else. I'm pleased for her. But it still doesn't mean I've forgiven her for preventing me from attending an important social function with my new peers!

DECEMBER

Tuesday, Dec. 7th, 8.30 p.m.

What a mad week – way too much work. But at least things have got a bit more normal at last. (Ha! That's a laugh! 'Normal' ceased to exist when we moved here.) Had a bit of a heart to heart with Mum today. She brought me a cup of peppermint tea, a sure sign that she had something to say. Apparently Poppy told her how important the invitation to Kate's was to me. I felt awful when she told me how special we are to her, but her time is so precious that we should spend it together whenever we can. She's right. I can't believe I've been sulking with her for over a week! I gave her a big hug and said sorry for being such a brat, and that I thought James seemed really nice.

Then, totally out of the blue, she asked me about Christmas! Never in a million years did I expect her to ask me what I wanted to do or what I think she should do! I was nervous of upsetting her and I could have lied, but seeing as she'd opened up to me . . . I said I wanted to go home, to see Dad and Carmel and everyone. I could tell she was disappointed, but it's the truth. She told me to ring Dad, but he was out. I hope he rings back soon.

Wednesday, Dec. 8th, 7.00 p.m.

I just don't believe it! Why is my life such a joke? Dad finally rang back, and I told him the news. I could tell by his voice that he wasn't expecting it! I certainly wasn't expecting him to say what he did either. He said he'd love me to spend the whole holidays with him, but he thinks it'd be for the best if I just went on Boxing Day for a few days! A few days? What can I do in a few days? How am I going to be able to catch up with everyone and everything in a few days? He said I should be here for Christmas Day and New Year, at home with Mum. This isn't home! He told me it was time I started to think of it as exactly that. I know what it is: he just doesn't want me there. This is just one big nightmare! I've got to ring Carmel. She's the only one who understands me.

Thursday, Dec. 9th, 8.25 p.m.

I wanted to stay off school, but Mum wouldn't let me. My eyes were all red and puffy from crying after talking to Carmel. The idea was that she'd cheer me up, but even she agrees with Dad! Everyone is turning against me! She said it would be plenty of time, but a few days will never be enough.

Then, just when I think things can't get any worse, they do. At lunch Bryony was talking about her New Year's Eve party. By the sound of it, everyone's going. I pretended not to be listening. She has got no manners! She ignored me completely and leaned right across me to ask Kate if she could go. Kate didn't answer her. She looked at me and asked if I fancied it. Bryony's face dropped! I was so tempted to say yes, but I didn't. I could feel the tears starting to well up. But I couldn't cry in front of the cool crowd! No way! Instead, I lied. I lied to Kate, my one and only friend here. I told her I'd be going 'back home' to Carmel's fancy dress party. The lies just flowed! I almost believed myself. I felt terrible lying to Kate, especially when she started asking me where the party was, had I decided what costume I wanted, would Poppy make it for me . . . Then she told me she'd miss me! I felt even worse when Richard tried to talk me into staying here, but by then I couldn't go back on it. I'm awful. I don't deserve friends when I treat people like that! Still, at least I didn't look like a friendless, desperate charity case in front of Bryony.

Friday, Dec. 10th, 6.30 p.m.

Richard invited me along for pizza tonight with 'the gang'. I didn't particularly want to go. I still feel down about the party and guilty about lying to them all. But Mum persuaded me. In fact, I'd go so far as to say she forced me to go! She reminded me of the good time I'd missed at Kate's, and that if I want to fit in here, I can't turn down any invitations! I might be bad-minded, but I bet it's only because she wants the house to herself for the night!

Saturday, Dec. 11th, 11.20 a.m.

We had a pretty good time last night, but everyone was talking about Bryony's party. I wanted to tell Kate the truth, but I couldn't. I've dug this hole for myself and I can't get out of it now.

Monday, Dec. 13th, 4.30 p.m.

Only just over a week left in school. I can't believe it's gone so fast. This time last year, we were getting all excited at the thought of breaking up. I'm not even bothered this year.

I've not bought a single Christmas present yet. I've not really had time, with Mum always working late and me having to look after Dylan. But she did give me a generous advance on my pocket money because of all the extra baby-sitting I've done. I think there might have been some extra thrown in for enduring night after night of Poppy's burned offerings too! Maybe I should ask Kate to go late-night shopping after t'ai chi this evening.

Tuesday, Dec. 14th, 10.00 p.m.

Whooh! What a great decision it was to start these classes. I had a brilliant time last night. It was the last lesson of the year, so everyone suggested we go into the leisure centre café for a coffee. Most of the people who go are getting on a bit, but there are a couple of younger ones. They seem a nice bunch too. One or two are even weirder than I am! But what made it even better was I saw Saul! He was there with a gang, who unfortunately, dare I say it, looked like typical train-spotters!

He gave me a shy little smile when he noticed me and asked how my bruises were! Ahh! He's so cute! I told him they were a nice shade of purple now. I thought he was going so I said bye, but he asked me what class I'd been to. I wasn't sure what his reaction would be – what would happen if he told Richard and Richard told Bryony? I made him promise not to laugh and told him.

He actually seemed pretty impressed, so I asked him what he did. I didn't have a clue. The crowd he was with hardly looked the skateboarding type! He's an amateur geologist! He goes to this group that meets in a room behind the leisure centre to examine and discuss rocks!! That's why he liked my pendant so much! How boring! And they say you can never judge a book by its cover. He plays guitar in a band, skateboards, listens to heavy metal and loves rocks! No wonder he wants to keep it quiet. It's almost as dorky as t'ai chi! I hope he isn't psychic too because he certainly seemed to know what I was thinking. He turned round and shuffled off. I think I heard a little 'see you' when I said bye. Oh, I hope I've not blown it with him now!

Wednesday, Dec. 15th, 10.30 p.m.

The end of term is officially on its way. The Sixth Formers did a talent show with some of the teachers as surprise guests. They were really funny! I could never have imagined Dr Monkman and a few others doing an impression of the best boy band in the world! Cringeable!

I asked Kate if they have some kind of school disco or Christmas party. She said that because the school's so big, people just tend to do their own thing. When I asked what they had planned, she said we are going ice-skating! 'We'? I wonder if I'm on the guest-list this time? I didn't bother to ask. I know I should have, Kate's bound to invite me, but I just feel that Bryony wants to exclude me from everything.

To be honest, I don't want to be around Bryony any more anyway. She is such a cow. I spotted her on the way home being really mean to Jacqui. I'm not sure what it was about, but she had her in tears! And that's one of her friends! Frankly, I'm surprised she's got any friends at all!

Thursday, Dec. 16th, 10.20 p.m.

Well, I'm exhausted. Poppy picked Dylan up from school so I could go late-night shopping with Kate. I stupidly arranged to meet her in town after we'd changed and had some tea. I managed to get on the wrong bus and I found myself hopelessly lost around the side of the city centre that I never even knew existed! I couldn't believe it! We've been here for months now and I *still* don't know my way around. That's what I get for being confident! Thank god I had a helpful driver who gave me directions. This place is huge. But it did give me an opportunity to have a good look at all the Christmas decorations in the shops. They look amazing! I don't think I've ever seen so many lights and trees and grottoes before!

When I finally found Kate, she looked frozen. We went for a hot chocolate to warm her up and I ended up telling her about how nasty Bryony was to Jacqui yesterday. She wasn't surprised. She said that's why we were destined to be friends – because we're the only two people in the school who don't go along with any whim of Bryony's! That's why she 'adopted' me in the first place. She knew I'd be a decent, caring and loyal friend from the moment she saw me! Ahh! She's such a sweetie! And thank god she did take me under her wing. I can't imagine how awful things would be here without her. I'm lucky to have her as a friend.

I'm all spent out now. Kate showed me even more new shops, so I bought the majority of the presents I went for. This place is a shopaholic's paradise! I must admit, listening to all those carol singers and seeing umpteen Santas has made me feel a bit Christmassy at last!

Friday, Dec. 17th, 11.10 p.m.

I stayed in tonight. Mum wanted us to put up the decorations and do the tree together. She's bought loads of new ornaments and things. We had a nice evening doing everything, but now I feel really down. It's all so different. Nothing is ever going to be the same again. Nothing.

Sunday, Dec. 19th, 3.30 p.m.

We've had a whole weekend of wrapping presents, putting up tinsel and Christmas lights. The house looks fantastic. Actually, the whole neighbourhood looks wonderful. I should be getting as excited as Dylan, but I can't. I miss home.

Monday, Dec. 20th, 9.50 p.m.

I hardly knew what to do with myself this evening without my t'ai chi. I haven't even got any homework because we break up on Wednesday. It's the ice-skating night then, too. Kate asked if I've ever been before. I was too surprised to tell her that's all we ever did back home at weekends. I wonder how different it's going to be here though?

Wednesday, Dec. 22nd, 11.50 p.m.

Phew! I'd forgotten what hard work skating is. I'd also forgotten what good times we used to have back home. I had to keep reminding myself that I wasn't with Carmel and the gang. But, we had a really good night! Exhausting, but good. That is until it was time to go. Bryony told me to have a 'fun time at the fancy dress party'. Then she said, 'Don't eat too much jelly and ice cream,' and made some sarcastic comment about me being right at home judging by the clothes I normally wear. Richard told me to ignore her – again! He said if my party plans changed, to come along to Bryony's. Kate made me promise to ring her if I got back in time. I can't believe I still haven't told her, but as more time passes, it gets harder. I know now that I'll be desperate to ring her, but I can't!

Thursday, Dec. 23rd, 8.45 p.m.

The first morning of the Christmas hols. Normally I'd say 'hooray', but what have I got to look forward to? A Christmas in a new house, a measly few days with Dad and my friends and a New Year baby-sitting Dylan most probably.

I spent most of the day cleaning and then had another argument with Mum. Could this get any worse? But at least this time we made up quickly, and I guess she's made me understand how hard it'd be for Dad to say we should stay here. She said he probably wants us with him more than anything – but more importantly, he wants us to settle down here. Once he knows we are happy, he will be too.

Saturday, Dec. 25th, 11.58 p.m.

Happy Christmas! We have had a wonderful time today! Dylan woke us all up at four this morning, screaming that Father Christmas had been! I just wanted to roll over and go back to sleep, but Poppy dragged me to his room so we could watch him open his presents. He was *so* excited, bless him! He must've only had about three hours' sleep! I left him playing and went back to bed. I wasn't there for long when Mum woke me up. She'd brought me breakfast in bed, and one little present on the tray. It was this lovely set of rune stones. She said that she hoped they'd tell me what a bright future we've got here. I've spent all day reading up on them. They are so interesting!

We had a lovely lunch, just the four of us. Mum had gone to loads of trouble. Then, we rang Dad. I was expecting to get all melancholic, but it was great. He asked if we'd got our bags packed and said that he couldn't wait to see us! Neither can I. I can't believe this time tomorrow I'll be there.

Then, just before we had our Christmas pud, there was a loud knock on the door! There was James dressed as Father Christmas and Brad as an elf! We couldn't stop laughing! After all my moaning, I've had a great day. It was different, but great none the less.

Sunday, Dec. 26th, 9.00 p.m.

Well. After hours of travelling, we are here at Dad's. We all hugged him for ages. It's wonderful to be back! I can't wait to see Carmel.

Monday, Dec. 27th, 11.30 a.m.

I don't believe this. I rang Carmel first thing this morning, and she's got to go to her gran's. I mean! I know she's old and everything, but it's not every day your best friend comes back home! When I rang around the others, I found out Mary and Lucy have gone away, and everyone else was doing 'family stuff'. I'm meeting them tomorrow now, but this just isn't the home-coming I expected.

Tuesday, Dec. 28th, 9.35 a.m.

I feel a bit better today. I ended up doing 'family stuff' myself yesterday and spent most of the day with Dad. Just me and him. It was lovely. I've missed him so much. (Poppy had gone off gallivanting with the old crowd and Kay was looking after Dylan, or was it the other way round? He's fascinated with her bump! She's really showing now. Just think! In a few months I'll be a big sister again!)

Dad and I had a big heart to heart. I told him all about how hard it is fitting in back there and how much I missed it here. He said it's bound to take time. That's why he thought I should spend Christmas Day and New Year there. He wants me to try to move on, and learn not to live in the past but look forward to the future. He also asked if I'd forgiven him for not letting me come sooner. I have now, actually. Him and Mum were right after all. Of course, I still missed him, but at least I'm here now.

I'm off round to see Carmel in a few minutes! I'm so excited! Actually, I feel quite nervous. I hope nothing's changed between us.

Wednesday, Dec. 29th, 2.00 p.m.

Oh, why aren't things ever straightforward for me? It was lovely to see Carmel again, but very weird. Things aren't quite the same any more. It was almost as though we were both on our best behaviour! I don't want to be like that with my best friend! The whole place feels different. At least it's not just me. Poppy said the same thing. And I know that it'll take time before things feel more normal. I'm just not so sure they ever will again.

11.00 p.m.

I had butterflies in my stomach waiting for everyone outside the pizza place this afternoon. (We've booked a table for tomorrow.) It was great to see them all! But when they started asking me all my news, it really made me aware that I'm not part of all this any more.

It freaked me out when we walked round our old haunts. It was such a strange feeling, especially when we got close to our old street. I really wanted to see our house again, but I couldn't stop crying when I did! There's a whole bunch of strangers living in my home! After a few minutes, Carmel managed to calm me down. I could've been depressed for the rest of the day, but the gang went to so much trouble for me. We had tea at Carmel's, took Lucky (who is still the world's cutest dog) for a walk round the park and met up with a few kids from school. Then we had to ask around to see whose mum or dad could give us a lift to the ice rink. It was odd – I've actually got used to being able to hop on a bus whenever I want to. I think Dad knows what he's talking about after all. I am starting to feel settled in the new town. I just hadn't realised it.

I can't wait for tomorrow night!

Thursday, Dec. 30th, 11.45 p.m.

Whooh! We have had the best time tonight! It was exactly like it always was! Mary and Lucy were back, so the old gang was complete once more! I've missed everyone so much. I can't bear to think I've got to go back tomorrow. One thing's for certain, I'm going to make sure I visit every school holidays, especially with the baby coming too. Carmel even suggested coming to visit us.

Oh my god! I've just realised. It's New Year's Eve tomorrow. I'm going to be bored out of my head while everyone dances the night away at Bryony's party. Once again, I come down to earth with a bump!

Friday, Dec. 31st, 6.30 p.m.

Here I am. Back again. It feels like I've never been away. I'm already missing everyone. It's just like the first time we left. Oh god. I hate New Year's Eve!

7.15 p.m.

Argh! What am I doing? I was sitting in my room, surrounded by chocolates, ready for an action-packed night watching TV when Mum came in and asked what my plans were. I told her I was staying in. She asked if none of my friends were having parties! Ha! Friends! I told her yes, but I'd not been invited! Then, I started crying – yet again. (It feels like that's all I've been doing lately!) And we had a good chat – yet again! What's going on? Me and Mum keep getting along these days! I don't know what's scarier. That, or the fact I let her talk me into ringing Kate! She was so excited that I'd changed my plans. I can't believe I'm going to gatecrash Bryony's party! Well. Here goes!

JANUARY

Saturday, Jan. 1st, 1.10 p.m.

I definitely should've consulted my rune stones before I went out! I wonder if they could've predicted what was going to happen? I certainly couldn't rely on my sixth sense this time!

Where shall I start? I was a nervous wreck by the time I got to Kate's. And when we arrived at the party, my legs were like jelly – without the ice cream! Kate kept telling me not to worry, but she was invited. I wasn't!

Bryony was livid when she saw me! I thought she was going to kick me out herself, until Richard came to the rescue. He said he'd invited me! That shut her up then, but she got me on my own, of course. She asked if I'd been to the fancy dress party already. I couldn't work out what she meant until I saw the way she was looking at my black beaded skirt and chiffon top. I bit my tongue and said Richard would've been so upset if I hadn't at least shown my face! She didn't look too happy when she went away, but I started to relax a bit. In fact, I'd go so far as to say I started to enjoy myself. It was really nice to see Kate again – and a couple of the others. It made me realise that things have got better since I first arrived – and I have actually got some friends!

I even felt brazen enough to dance. Kate and I were happily grooving away – and then I spotted Bryony. She was giving me the worst daggers yet. I felt so self-conscious! But her timing couldn't have been worse! The smoochie records came on and everything went into slow motion! It was like being in a film. The dance floor literally cleared, and there was Saul. I just knew he was going to ask me to dance! How could I in front of Bryony? That would've pleased her no end and given her more ammunition to embarrass me with at every opportune moment! I'm so ashamed – I practically laughed at him! I was so abrupt. I can't believe how cruel I was! He's so sweet too!

Kate made me feel even worse! She asked what I was playing at and she thought I really liked him. I do! But yet again I was possessed – I lied and told Kate I'd decided he was too young for me. Where did I get that from? Then she goes and tells me that she's been egging him on all night to ask me! She thought she would be doing us both a favour by playing Cupid. I'm such a cow! How could I do that to them both? I make Kate look ridiculous and especially poor Saul – and in front of all his friends and brother, too!

His brother! Oh, god! Why did I bother going? After the Saul fiasco I rushed off to ring Mum to pick me up, and Richard was right by the phone. My stomach was in a knot. In one night, I'd managed to offend two of the best friends I've got here, and waiting for Richard's protective big-brother reaction nearly killed me. Now I wish it had! That was preferable to what he did do. He kissed me – and just as Bryony walked in on us!

She had hysterics! I was out of the house before I knew it. I think I had a lucky escape too. I thought she was going to kill me! Richard pulled her off me and then he disappeared. I think I must've been in shock. There's no way I'd have walked off on my own in the middle of the night otherwise! It was only when Kate caught up with me that I realised I was halfway down the street. Thank god she came. I could've ended up anywhere! She was brilliant! She gave me a shoulder to cry on and shepherded me home. But I was totally shocked when she told me she had seen it all coming! How come I hadn't?

What did I do in a past life? It must've been pretty bad. What a wonderful start to the New Year!

Monday, Jan. 3rd, 11.00 a.m.

I've only just left my room. I think Mum thought I was hibernating. I wish I could! Anything rather than face everyone in school next week!

Friday, Jan. 7th, 3.30 p.m.

Thank god for Kate! She's been round to cheer me up. Well, she tried at least. I asked her if she'd heard how Bryony was. I feel so bad for her. She must hate me.

God! She's going to give me hell in school. Why me? Why couldn't Richard have fancied someone else? And how dare he just kiss me like that! Where did he get the idea from in the first place? I mean, I didn't give him any encouragement whatsoever. Or did I? Maybe I've been giving him the wrong signals. Perhaps I have been giving him the come-on without even knowing! *Argh!*

Saturday, Jan. 8th, 5.00 p.m.

Mum and Poppy have been doing their best to cheer me up. Poppy still thinks the whole thing is hysterically funny though! She won't think that when she sees me black and blue next week after Bryony and her crew get their hands on me! Oh god!

Sunday, Jan. 9th, 11.15 p.m.

I feel sick. My stomach is in about twenty knots. I don't even think I felt this bad when it was my first day at school here. Oh! I wish tomorrow was just over with. *Déjà vu!*

Monday, Jan. 10th, 4.30 p.m.

I was right to worry! I am officially a social outcast. I've been treated like some scarlet woman! It's not fair! I haven't done anything. Everyone hates me. Well, everyone except Kate and – surprisingly – Nina and Rachael. Either they haven't heard what went on or they don't care, but I feel even more guilty now for being mean to them. That's it now. I'm determined to be nice to people who are nice to me, whether they're cool or not. Bryony's gang run hot and cold, depending on what she tells them to be! I just can't believe I got taken in by it!

Kate literally had to drag me through the school gates this morning. When I saw Bryony and the gang waiting for me, my legs went to jelly. I tried to ignore them, like Kate said. It wasn't that easy though. They called me names and shouted all kinds of abuse! It was horrible. Why are they being so mean? I haven't even done anything! And to think I'd actually started to think that some of them were my friends!

It took all my concentration not to cry and run off. Thank god I didn't. Imagine how that would've looked! If it hadn't been for Kate . . . Well. She was just wonderful. She had such a go at them. From what I remember, she was telling them to grow up, and if they did want to pick on someone, it should be Richard. One of them said they would once they saw him. He must be lying low. I wish I could! It's OK for him. He's in another year! But I have to take all the flack!

Bryony herself was frighteningly calm. But then I bumped into her in the loo. Kate had only left my side for a few seconds as well! I panicked. I half expected her to knock me out, but I didn't give her the chance. I just blurted out that I was sorry *and* completely innocent! I tried to explain that I'd done absolutely nothing to encourage Richard, and that I only ever saw him as a friend. She just didn't want to hear it. She eyeballed me for ages and called me a liar! She said I'd been flirting with him since I came here! Then she told me I was welcome to him and stormed out in floods of tears. I don't think I can stand much more of this.

Tuesday, Jan. 11th, 5.00 p.m.

I tried to pretend I had flu this morning, but Mum wasn't having any of it. She told me I needed to see this through, and that it'll all blow over shortly. I doubt it.

Thursday, Jan. 13th, 10.15 p.m.

Two more wonderful days! I'm getting the silent treatment now instead of verbal abuse. Kate said it is a definite step in the right direction! That was until we were going home. I thought there was going to be World War Three! We only bumped into Richard and his mates outside the newsagent's! I didn't want to go near him, but Kate didn't give me much choice. She dragged me across the road, screaming his name at the top of her voice. She was like a mad woman! I've never seen her like that before! I tried to convince her to leave well alone, but she said it'd only take a minute, and it was better to get it over and done with now. I didn't argue! *I* was frightened of her, let alone Richard!

It was so awkward! I felt angry and embarrassed at the same time. I couldn't even look at him! If lightning had struck me, I'd have been grateful. I think he might have been too! Kate made a holy show of him. Actually, it must've looked quite funny to passers-by: this tiny, wild woman screaming at this tall, blushing older boy and me standing there, like a spare part! It wasn't funny at the time though. I just wanted to get away. But I'm glad now that she made me stay. She said exactly what I wanted to myself, but I just couldn't find the words! It was along the lines of her thinking he was our friend and only a coward would let me take the blame for what *he'd* done.

He was really quiet at first, then he said sorry and he would never have done it if he hadn't been drinking. He sounded sorry too. He said he should've realised I'd be getting hassle and promised to set the record straight. I believed him, but I had to make him realise exactly what he's done! I even managed to look him right in the eye! I told him it wasn't easy being the new kid, that I'd only just started to be accepted by everyone, but now I'm back to square one. My face was burning up, but I did it! I'm rather proud of myself, actually, for telling him. Kate said she's sure he regrets it all and is bound to keep his promise. I certainly hope so.

Sunday, Jan. 16th, 8.20 p.m.

Kate has just called round to tell me the good news. She saw Richard in town and he'd been to see Bryony. He told her the whole story – that he surprised me, and that I'd not expected or encouraged or returned his kiss! Excellent! There's just one thing . . . I know I'm being a pessimist as usual, but I can't believe she'd just accept it like that. Kate said he'd insisted it was all his fault, but will she believe him? I wonder if I would if I were in her shoes? I mean, it does take two to kiss – but I was so shocked, it was a second or two before I realised what was happening and moved away. By then it was too late! Ah well, I'll know tomorrow, that's for sure.

Monday, Jan. 17th, 6.00 p.m.

So much for my own private agony aunt! Poppy hasn't got a clue! 'You're always worrying unnecessarily, Jaz. Loosen up!' she says. God! How wrong could she be? Bryony's been nastier than ever. I knew she wouldn't believe Richard! She told me my new boyfriend had been defending my honour. I tried to argue with her, but she told me we deserved each other and turned her back on me! This is terrible! When am I going to get a break around here?

Thursday, Jan. 20th, 4.40 p.m.

Mrs Wallis has asked me to represent my year group in a national debating competition! I'd love to, but she asked me right in front of the whole class. Bryony started being sarcastic straight away, and I just bottled it. Kate went mad with me for saying no! I'm mad with myself, but I just can't do it. They make my life a misery already – I can't bear to give them more ammunition . . .

Saturday, Jan. 22nd, 6.30 p.m.

Mum took me shopping to cheer me up. Even that didn't work. Then I rang Carmel and Dad to see if that would work. Listening to him going on about how much Kay's bump is wriggling about now didn't even improve my mood. My life stinks. Will it ever get any better?

Sunday, Jan. 23rd, 3.00 p.m.

I've spent all day doing homework. I think I need a break. Maybe I could call on Kate. I could do with talking this debate thing through with her. I mentioned it to Carmel yesterday. She thinks I'm stupid not to do it. I felt ashamed when I told her why. I knew she'd tell me off for worrying about what other people think! It's OK for her, though. She's not bearing the brunt of Bryony's nastiness. I am. And the truth is, I'm just not the person I used to be. No. There's no way I can do it. No way.

Monday, Jan. 26th, 7.40 p.m.

How gullible am I? I say one thing one day, then do the complete opposite the next! I still don't know how Kate managed to talk me into it. She'd even asked Mrs Wallis to give her until Monday before she looked for my replacement! Talk about confident! She knows me that well already. I'm such a push-over. She is amazing though! I hardly even noticed she was doing it! Both her and Mrs Wallis seem to think I'll be perfect for the team, so who am I to argue with them? I'm glad I changed my mind.

I shouldn't be so worried about what other people think of me. I don't care how many of the cool crowd call me a goody-goody. I'm not going to let them or Bryony put me off. Like Kate said, she's probably just jealous anyway! And it's about time I stopped trying to impress her. Let's face it, I'm never going to be cool or hip enough to be one of her crowd anyway. I'm sick of trying to be something I'm not. And I'm sick of their bitchiness and shallowness. I've got my own friends now. I don't need to ingratiate myself with Bryony's little gang any more! From now on, I'm concentrating on me – and what I want and what makes me happy.

Tuesday, Jan. 25th, 8.15 p.m.

Wow! This is so exciting! I've only just got in now after our first debate meeting. There's one person from every year group. I didn't meet them all because one was off sick, but they seem a nice bunch. If nothing else, at least I'm getting to recognise a few more faces! I'm trying to imagine how it'll feel being in front an audience of hundreds in the town hall! Mum's already deciding what outfit to wear and we haven't even chosen a topic yet. We've got a week to come up with something we feel strongly about. Poppy suggested I do something about the New Age movement. It's a pretty good suggestion, but I'm sure there could be something even better. I'll have to get thinking!

Wednesday, Jan. 26th, 4.30 p.m.

This is great! I feel like a new person! Bryony found out I was on the team. She started to put her acid tongue into gear, but I just cut her dead! Me! Ha! I told her to save her funny comments for someone who cares! She didn't like it. Not one bit. She tried to start a full-blown argument, but I just walked away. Me! I'm amazed even now that I did it! Kate said Bryony's face was a picture. I've been buzzing ever since. I feel like a new woman!

Friday, Jan. 28th, 11.50 p.m.

Kate and I have been baby-sitting Dylan while Mum and James went out. It must be serious, even though Mum insists it's not. They've been together for ages now. Perhaps they can have a double wedding with Poppy and Brad! *Urgh!* All this romance makes me sick. Ha! The irony is Kate and I spent hours in the video shop choosing a slushy film to watch. I wonder what the rest of the Friday night gang got up to? I never thought I'd say this, but the truth is, I don't care! And it feels great to say that!

Saturday, Jan. 29th, 5.20 p.m.

I told Dad all about the debate. He said if I let him know the date, he'll try to get some time off work to come and watch me! Brilliant!

Sunday, Jan. 30th, 10.30 p.m.

This time two weeks ago, I was worried sick. It's weird, but now I'm almost looking forward to seeing Bryony. Maybe the more I stand up to her the better I'll feel. Or maybe not, but I'm going to have fun trying out the theory!

Monday, Jan. 31st, 9.10 p.m.

Just got back from a great t'ai chi lesson. My karma feels more recharged every time I go! I didn't see Saul though. Either he's unwell or he's avoiding me. God! I'm going to have to face him some time. I wish it were sooner rather than later! He's the only part of this mess that hasn't been sorted. I still feel rotten and actually, I quite miss him . . .

FEBRUARY

Tuesday, Feb. 1st, 9.30 p.m.

My life is just one amazing coincidence after another! I wonder what the chances are exactly of the missing person from the debate team being Saul? It's amazing! My jaw almost dropped to the floor when I saw him. He wasn't surprised though. He looked like he was expecting to see me, actually.

I gave him a nervous smile and got a pretty unenthusiastic one back. But I wasn't just going to leave it there! I'd had enough torture! So I asked him why he missed his geology class last night. I couldn't think of anything else to say. 'Hi, Saul. How's your life been since I publicly humiliated you?' wouldn't have sounded quite as good! He said he's had flu. I hope it was. I couldn't bear to think he's been off, avoiding people, because of me. I apologised for being so rude at the party. He told me not to worry and that he's used to his brother getting all the girls! Aw! That didn't make me feel any better! He said he was only joking and there were no hard feelings, but I'm not too sure. I insisted there was nothing going on between Richard and me. Apparently, that's what Richard keeps telling everyone. I didn't get a chance to ask him if he believed him.

Thankfully, Mrs Wallis cut our conversation short. She wanted our suggestions. There were loads, but Saul came up with the best. I couldn't have picked a better one if I'd tried. The topic's going to be 'Fitting In'. It'll be about how difficult it is being a teenager, coping with everyday pressures. This is going to be excellent! I've got so many ideas I don't know where to start!

Friday, Feb. 4th, 11.20 p.m.

Between all this homework and debate practice I'm exhausted, but it's fun. The team are all really nice.

I'd even go so far as to say that I think Saul is getting more comfortable around me. I know I'm getting more comfortable around him again.

Sunday, Feb. 6th, 6.00 p.m.

Mum is amazed how serious I am about this debate. I've been working on it all weekend. I'm ordering my tickets tomorrow. Dad was telling me how much he's looking forward to coming. It's not as much as I am! I can't wait! It's going to be so exciting!

Friday, Feb. 11th, 5.00 p.m.

Where has this week gone? I can't believe that we've only got another week before the real thing. The practices have been great. Saul is definitely the star of the show. He's so quick and has the perfect answer to any question. There's no awkwardness between us at all now. I think he must've forgiven me. Actually, he doesn't seem the type to hold a grudge. He's so nice. And so much fun. The more I get to know him, the more I like him. He's got the driest sense of humour, but can be completely wacky too. He reminds me of Richard, but he's much more of a free spirit. And considering he's younger than me (by only a few months as it happens), he can be so mature and deep when the mood takes him! I really like him!!

Saturday, Feb. 12th, 2.30 p.m.

Kate tried to drag me out shopping today, but there was no way I could go. I've had too much to do working out a weekend's itinerary for Dad's visit! So Kate's going to join me later on instead – I'm meeting up with a few of the gang from t'ai chi. I'm sure she'll like them.

I am so excited about Dad coming. I can't wait to show him round. Things are going so well at the moment. Maybe too well. Even Bryony's been keeping her distance these days. Actually, I feel really sorry for her. She looks so miserable. So does Richard. Saul was telling me what a grouch he's been. I don't know why the two of them haven't kissed and made up yet. It's obvious they want to.

Monday, Feb. 14th, 11.20 p.m.

Had *two* mystery Valentine's cards! How exciting! I was terrified for a moment that one was from Richard, but I'm sure it wasn't. He wouldn't be that dumb – he's been really normal ever since we had 'words'. But I'm sure that one of them was from Saul! I bumped into him tonight. I'd been considering missing t'ai chi because I've got so much to do, but I went anyway. We went for a burger afterwards. I could have sworn he was blushing at first, and he was a bit shy, but I just acted normal and pretended I'd not noticed anything. I really don't want things to get awkward, or spoil anything! We've been spending so much time together lately, but I never get fed up of seeing him. I think Carmel thinks I fancy him, but it's not like that. He's cute and everything, but I just enjoy his company. In fact, I'd go so far as to say he's just a good friend! Wow! I can't believe how good it feels to say that! Just think, if it hadn't been for Kate, Bryony would've put me off and I'd still be as miserable and friendless as before. Meeting Kate and now doing this debate has changed my life! I finally have some really good friends here! And the crowd from t'ai chi. (We all had a brill time on Saturday night.) On top of all that, I feel like my old self again. Hooray!

Thursday, Feb. 17th, 10.50 p.m.

I'm getting nervous now after talking to Dad. I know him being here is going to make me even *more* nervous, but it'll be great too. At least I'm not going to see him before the debate, only after. He's going to have to go straight there because of the time it starts. Ooh! I'm so excited! I just know I'm not going to get a wink of sleep! And this is only the regional competition! If we win this, we have to travel for the national finals! Can you imagine how terrifying *that* would be?? I wouldn't sleep for a month!

Friday, Feb. 18th, 8.00 p.m.

He never came! What's going on? I just can't believe he'd let me down like that. So much for all my plans! And after we won too! We had the best time, but he's spoiled it all. Why would he do that? Why didn't he even ring? I can't believe it – my own father! There's no way I'm going to sit here and mope. Saul's invited me out with the team to celebrate and Mum's just talked me into going. He's not ruining my day!

Saturday, Feb. 19th, 8.30 a.m.

Whooh! I've got a new sister! Wow! That sounds so weird! They're going to call her Maria. Ah! I can't wait to see her. I hardly got any sleep last night (again!). Neither did Dylan. He's going wild at the thought of being a big brother. It's been a bit weird though. Poppy and I are really excited, but we don't want to show it too much in front of Mum. She said she's really pleased for them both, and I'm sure she genuinely is, but at the same time, I bet she's thinking about 'the old days' and when we were born.

I'm annoyed. If I'd have gone home after the debate I would have heard Dad's message on the answerphone. Then I could've celebrated instead of moaning all night about him letting me down and forgetting me. God! How embarrassing! It's a good job

Saul's so understanding. I knew there must've been a good reason for Dad not to come. I was thinking badly of him and all the time he was at Kay's bedside in the hospital. I've got a new sister! Ooh!

Sunday, Feb. 20th, 9.10 p.m.

What a mad weekend! I finally spoke to Dad. He sounded so excited! He said the baby reminds him of me when I was born! I really wish I could see her now instead of waiting two weeks. Then again, I suppose it's not that long. Wow! It all feels unreal still. It sounded strange telling Carmel that I'm a big sister again! And Maria's an Aquarius too! It couldn't be any better. We are going to be so compatible! And even in all the excitement Dad remembered the debate. He was so upset to have missed it, especially after Mum told him how wonderful I was! Mum! Proud of me! That's a first! Yes. It's been a very unusual weekend, that's for sure.

She wouldn't be proud of me being devious though. Well. It's all for a good cause. Saul's had enough of Richard. He's making life at their house unbearable. Saul's convinced everything would be normal if Richard and Bryony got back together! He really put me on the spot. I couldn't say no! Saul's been a real friend to me, so I've got to repay the favour. What am I doing? This is Bryony we are talking about here! The trouble is, he doesn't realise how serious the clash of personalities between us has become. I'm going to need some help with this one. I wonder if Kate would be interested in playing Cupid too?

Monday, Feb. 21st, 10.40 p.m.

My t'ai chi lesson was cancelled! I almost laughed at Saul when he asked me to sit in on his class instead. But I didn't laugh, thank god. Upsetting him at New Year's Eve was more than enough for one lifetime. But I genuinely thought he was joking at first! He wasn't. I didn't want to hurt his feelings, even though the thought of sitting looking through magnifying glasses at a bunch of rocks hardly appealed, so I found myself saying yes. I was cringing going in with him. All the time I was worrying about anyone seeing me. Then it hit me! I was becoming like Bryony again! Ugh! The thought of that snapped me out of it! I actually quite enjoyed it. It was pretty interesting to learn about the physical characteristics as well as the spiritual, healing properties of stones. OK. So geology isn't the coolest hobby in the world, but so what?

Tuesday, Feb. 22nd, 5.00 p.m.

We managed to talk Kate into joining Operation Cupid. She took a bit of convincing, mind you. I think she's as cautious as me about getting Richard involved with Bryony again. But the more I see of him, the more I agree with Saul. I'm doing this for him, not her. And even though I didn't do anything wrong, it feels right that I should be the one to get them back together again. After all, if I hadn't been such a fantastically gorgeous person, then they wouldn't have split up in the first place!

Wednesday, Feb. 23rd, 7.50 p.m.

The baby is home from hospital already! Dad says she's a little angel. She definitely must take after me! After today, I am seriously wondering why we are going to any trouble at all for Bryony! She can be such a cow. Totally out of the blue, she asked me who my favourite band was. I was sucked in yet again. I actually thought she was being nice and making polite conversation so I told her. And she goes, 'Oh, I thought you'd like *rock* music!' and starts bitching to her giggling cronies about my going to geology classes with my baby boyfriend, and how sad . . . etc, etc. It's actually getting rather boring now! What does Richard see in her? Maybe it's true what they say that opposites attract! If it wasn't for him being Saul's brother, and Saul believing in destiny, then I wouldn't be bothering.

Friday, Feb. 25th, 11.30 p.m.

It's amazing! It worked! Well, at least we got them together. We'll have to wait and see how the night went. I never thought it'd be so easy. Bryony must be at such a loose end since they broke up! Kate said she jumped at the chance of going to the cinema with us! I felt a bit cruel watching her waiting for us at the bus stop. It was so funny though when Richard's car pulled up. The two of them were trying so hard to pretend they hadn't spotted the other! They didn't know what was happening when Kate pushed Bry into the passenger seat! Their faces were pictures when we stood up from behind the wall and waved. You could literally see the penny drop! It was so funny! And we three had a good night out if nothing else.

Saturday, Feb. 26th, 11.40 p.m.

Well. We have spent all night discussing our future careers, and now we know. We are going to open a lonely hearts agency! Operation Cupid was a complete success. I can't wait to see Richard on Monday. I wonder what Bryony will have to say about it, if anything. I'm not holding my breath.

Sunday, Feb. 27th, 4.00 p.m.

Saul and I have just got back. He took me on a huge, long walk, miles away from town! It was just like being back in the country. I really miss all the trees and fields. But now I'm not used to all the exercise any more! I'm exhausted, but it was great fun! Who'd have thought I'd have enjoyed looking for rocks? It was a lovely afternoon! It certainly beats sitting in, watching Poppy and Brad or Mum and James stare into each other's eyes. Still – at least they are happy. And the strangest thing is, I think I am too.

Monday, Feb. 28th, 4.30 p.m.

I am amazed! You think you know someone . . . ! Wow! Bryony actually apologised to me! OK. Richard may very well have put her up to it, but nevertheless . . . ! She actually said sorry! And thanks! Wow!

Tuesday, Feb. 29th, 5.30 p.m.

Happy Leap Year! Bumped into Richard and Bryony today. He gave me this big hug! She didn't look too happy, but nothing near as bad as she used to if he did anything like that! They invited me bowling with the gang at the weekend as a thank you, but I said no. I don't know who was more surprised, me or them! It's not that I'm being funny with them or anything, but I don't want to be part of all that again. It was never 'me' anyway.

MARCH

Wednesday, Mar. 1st, 8.20 p.m.

I rang Carmel and told her I'll be going there at the
weekend. I can't wait to see the baby! I've bought
her a wind chime. You're never too young for Feng
Shui. Ooh! I'm so excited!

Friday, Mar. 3rd, 5.15 p.m.

Well. I'm all packed and ready to go. It's funny, but
for the first time, it doesn't feel like I'm going home,
but leaving home. Maybe I have fitted in after all . . .

Sunday 8.00 p.m.   Walking home, I said, "I don't think he's that keen on her. What sort of kiss do you think it was? Was there actual lip contact? Or was it lip to cheek, or lip to corner of mouth?"

"I think it was lip to corner of mouth, but maybe it was lip to cheek?"

"It wasn't **full-frontal snogging** though, was it?"

"No."

"I think she went for full-frontal and he converted it into lip to corner of mouth . . ."

Saturday 6.58 p.m.
Lindsay was wearing a thong! I don't understand **thongs** – what is the point of them? They just go up your bum, as far as I can tell!

Wednesday 10.30 p.m.
Mrs Next Door complained that **Angus** has been frightening their poodle again. He stalks it. I explained, "Well, he's a Scottish wildcat, that's what they do. They stalk their prey. I have tried to train him but he ate his lead."

*"This is very funny – very, very funny. I wish I had read this when I was a teenager, it really is **very funny**."* Alan Davies

Also available from Piccadilly Press, by
KATHRYN LAMB

Laetitia Alexandra Rebecca Fitt has more problems than just an odd name. Like three younger brothers (euk!), a baby sister, and an older sister with very strong views on life (Alex's). Having crazily busy parents may mean freedom – which is cool – but it also means they never notice Alex. Added to this, the love of Alex's life (Kevin in Year 12) doesn't know she exists. And then there's friends and parties . . .

By the author of the *Help!* series: *Help! My Family is Driving Me Crazy!, Help! My Social Life is a Mess!* and *Help! Let Me Out of Here!* and of the titles *Boywatching!, Girls are From Saturn Boys are From Jupiter* and *How to be Completely Cool*.

When Mr. 'hey, call me Dave'
Sissons suggests that 5B keep
a diary for a whole year,
reactions are decidedly mixed!
Yo! Diary! grants us exclusive
access to all areas of six very
different fifteen-year-old
minds:

Seb – the rebel and
'Spokesdood for a
generation';
Meera – a girl obsessed
with astrology;
Steven Stevens – so good
his parents named him twice;
Clare – the local neighbourhood Eco Warrior;
Mandy – Ms Personality and Karaoke Queen, and
Craig – convinced that he's the only virgin on the entire
planet.

Jonathan Meres has written a riveting and hilarious tale of
teenagers teetering on the edge of the millennium! It's a
story of changes, drama, love, intrigue and plenty of good
old angst! And that's just in the first week!

*"Meres' strong, irreverent characterisation and sharp humour
(he was a stand-up comedian with his own radio show) make
this a book that will achieve an effortless following."*
Publishing News

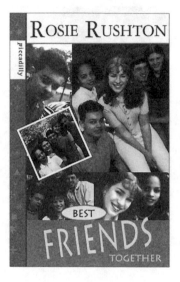

Who'd have thought that Chloë – cool, rich and so sophisticated – would have anything in common with Sinead, who longs for popularity?

And who'd have suspected the problems lurking beneath Jasmin's sparkling smile? And if we're talking about mysteries, then just who is Nick – the fit, supercool guy, but what is he hiding?

And what of Sanjay, who finds his computer so much more user-friendly than people? As five very different teenagers struggle to cope with their changing lives they fall into a friendship which surprises them all . . .

"*. . . five teenagers from very different backgrounds, the fun and drama of their lives is drawn with humour and sensitivity.*"
Pick of the Paperbacks – The Bookseller

If you would like more information about books available from Piccadilly Press and how to order them, please contact us at:

Piccadilly Press Ltd.
5 Castle Road
London
NW1 8PR

Tel: 020 7267 4492
Fax: 020 7267 4493